Christmas Wishes

adapted by *Bonnie Pinehurst*

based on the teleplay by *Kate Boutilier* and *Eryk Casemiro*

illustrated by *Kellee Riley*

LITTLE SIMON
An imprint of Simon & Schuster Children's Publishing Division
New York London Toronto Sydney
1230 Avenue of the Americas, New York, New York 10020
Holly Hobbie™ and related trademarks © 2006 Those Characters From Cleveland, Inc.
Used under license by Simon & Schuster, Inc. American Greetings with rose logo is a trademark of AGC, Inc.
All rights reserved, including the right of reproduction in whole or in part in any form.
LITTLE SIMON is a registered trademark of Simon & Schuster, Inc., and associated colophon is a trademark of Simon & Schuster, Inc.
Art direction and design by Cheshire Studio. Manufactured in the United States of America.
First Edition
2 4 6 8 10 9 7 5 3 1
ISBN-13: 978-1-4169-2796-9 ISBN-10: 1-4169-2796-4

The holiday spirit was taking over the small town of Clover. Lights sparkled, snowmen lined the walkways, and the cheerful voices of Holly Hobbie and her friends filled the chilly night air with Christmas carols.

"There's nothing I love more than singing with my best friends!" Holly proclaimed as she walked beside Aunt Jessie. "You're going to be great in the Christmas pageant!" said Carrie.

"I hope you're right," said Holly nervously. "Caroling feels so different from singing in a show. For some reason it feels like I'm helping people when we sing carols. But when I'm on stage, I feel like my stomach is full of butterflies."

Holly made an extra-special effort while leading the next carol at the Deegans' house.

"Thank you for the song," said Mrs. Deegan. "But it's getting late. We should be going to bed soon."

Her sons, Joey and Paul, hung their heads in disappointment. "Aww, Mom!"

Mrs. Deegan waved the boys inside, and Holly waved good-bye as her crew made their way down the driveway.

"Good night!" said Holly.

After warming up with some hot chocolate, Holly, Amy, and Carrie were ready for a secret meeting of the Hey Girls Club.

"I call this meeting to order," said Holly. "First we need to help the Deegans find their Christmas spirit. They looked so sad today."

"It's going to be tough," said Carrie. "This is their first Christmas without Mr. Deegan."

"We should do something to make it easier on them," said Holly excitedly.

"Hmm . . . what could we do?" asked Carrie.

The next afternoon the Hey Girls Club returned to the Deegans' house with a plate of warm cookies.

Mrs. Deegan opened the door as Joey and Paul crowded around her.

"Hi," said Holly cheerfully. "We thought you and the boys might like some snickerdoodles."

"That's sweet of you," said Mrs. Deegan with a smile.

"Are you going skating?" asked Joey.

"We are," replied Amy. "Do you want to come?" She turned to Mrs. Deegan. "We promise to watch them very closely."

Joey and Paul gazed at their mother with hopeful faces.

"Oh, okay," said Mrs. Deegan. "But come home before dark. Make sure to hold hands and listen to the girls."

"We'll be the best babysitters you've ever had!" promised Holly.

Everyone had a wonderful time at the skating pond.

"You look like a Christmas tree," Paul said to Carrie. They all laughed.

"Mommy said that we're not having a tree this year," said Joey.

When they were off the ice, Holly called Amy and Carrie into a Hey Girls Club huddle.

"I know how we could bring even more Christmas cheer to the Deegans," whispered Holly. "Let's bring them a tree and some homemade ornaments!"

"That's a great idea!" Amy and Carrie agreed. They whispered the Hey Girls Club secret phrase: Share a smile!

"This will *definitely* share a smile," said Holly.

On Christmas Day the Hey Girls Club carried a tree and decorations to the Deegans.

"Surprise!" the girls cheered as Mrs. Deegan came outside.

"You shouldn't have gone to so much trouble," said Mrs. Deegan quietly. "I don't want a Christmas tree this year."

"It was no trouble," said Holly. "We made most of the decorations, and my dad cut the tree."

"Thank you, but I don't want Christmas this year, and I don't want a tree," said Mrs. Deegan, wiping a tear from her cheek. She slowly closed the door.

"I think we've made things worse," said Holly sadly.

"Come on," said Carrie, leading the girls off the porch. "The pageant rehearsals are starting soon. Maybe the show will give us some new ideas to help the Deegans."

Holly, Carrie, and Amy went to Parish Hall to rehearse for the pageant. But no one was in the mood to practice.

"Mrs. Deegan used to be the most festive person in town," said Amy. "And when she sang a solo last year at the pageant, even cranky old Mr. Scranton smiled!"

"If only we could find a way to make the Deegans feel better," Holly said, scratching her chin.

"Too bad we couldn't find a way to make them join tonight's pageant," said Carrie. "But Mrs. Deegan wouldn't sing . . . unless it was an emergency."

Holly's eyes twinkled with excitement. "That's it!" she shouted. "This is a Christmas emergency! Hey Girls, follow me!"

The girls crossed their fingers behind their backs as they waited for Mrs. Deegan to open the door.

"Mrs. Deegan, we really need your help!" Amy stammered breathlessly.

"Holly came down with . . . with . . . with laryngitis . . .," said Carrie.

"And she can't sing the solo, so we need you to take her place," Amy chimed in.

"Because you sang it last year and you know how it should go," finished Carrie.

"Oh, Holly," said Mrs. Deegan, "this was your big night! I know how much you practiced."

"Please," croaked Holly.

Paul and Joey peeked out from behind their mother.

"We know you miss Daddy," said Joey softly. "We miss him too."

"But Daddy loved Christmas, and he would want you to be happy," added Paul.

Mrs. Deegan gave each of her boys a big hug. "Daddy *would* want us to be happy," she said. "And we all loved Christmas. Boys, get your coats! We have a show to save!"

Parish Hall bustled with noise as it filled with everyone ready to celebrate the Clover Christmas Pageant.

"Tonight Holly Hobbie's solo will be sung by last year's soloist, Mrs. Deegan," the pageant organizer announced.

The hall became silent as the spotlight turned to Mrs. Deegan standing center stage. She had a genuine smile on her face that people had not seen in many months. In a gentle voice she began the first verse of "O Holy Night."

"Wow," said Holly. "She sounds so beautiful."

"Holly?" said Aunt Jessie suspiciously. "I thought you lost your voice."

"Um . . . I think the Christmas spirit brought it back," Holly explained, smiling mischievously.

"I'm glad," said Aunt Jessie, hugging Holly tightly. "The Christmas spirit always has a way of making things better."

"What did I tell you?" said Holly. "This is *absolutely* a Christmas to remember!"